To err is hu̲

To arr is pirate.

To bee arrsome is dad.

To:_____ From:_____

_____

_____

_____

Pirate:
Another name for a naughty, knotty sailor.

A fool and his booty are soon parroted.

ISBN: 978-1-7361214-0-5

First edition 2023

Dad Jokes for Pirates

Who, What, When, Where and Why?

Q: Why couldn't the pirate say, 'Aye, aye, cap'n'?

A: Because he only had one eye.

Q: Which two football teams played in the pirate Super Bowl?

A: The Seahawks and the Buccaneers.

Q: What's orange and sounds like a parrot?

A: A carrot.

Q: Where do pirates go for a drink?

A: To the sandbar!

Q: What bank is a pirate's favorite bank?

A: The sandbank.

Q: Where did the pirate put his Halloween decoration?

A: In his front yarrrrrd!

Q: Why does it take pirates so long to learn the alphabet?

A: A and B are easy. But they can spend years at C.

Q: Why did the Captain run his ship aground?

A: Because he let his car-go!

Q: Why does the pirate carry his sword?

A: Because swords can't walk. Duh.

Q: Where did the pirate purchase his hook?

A: At the 2nd hand store.

Q: How come you can never call a pirate?

A: They always leave their phones off the hook.

Q: Which Halloween candy do pirates like the most?

A: Sweet Tarrrrrts.

Q: Where do pirates go for the bathroom?

A: The poop-deck!

Q: Why can't you take a picture of a pirate with a wooden leg?

A: Because a wooden leg doesn't take pictures!

Q: Which side of a parrot has the prettiest feathers?

A: The outside!

Q: Why was the pirate sad when his parrot left?

A: It gave him the cold shoulder!

Q: How much did the pirate pay for his hook and peg leg?

A: An arm and a leg.

Q: What has 8 legs, 8 arms, and 8 eyes?

A: 4 pirates.

Q: Where do pirates park their ships?

A: In the harrrrrrbor.

Q: Where can ye find a pirate who has lost his wooden leg?

A: Right where ye left him.

Q: Where are American pirates from?

A: Arrrkansas!

Q: What kind of phone does a pirate have?

A: An aye phone.

Q: What kind of a ship is most feared by pirates?

A: The Steady Relationship.

Q: What grades did the pirate get in school?

A: High Cs.

Q: Who was the first pirate?

A: Noah, the builder of the Arrrrk.

Q: What should you do when you see a coughing pirate?

A: Run, he probably has the SAAARRRRRRS!

Q: Which element on the periodic table does a pirate like the best?

A: Arrrrrrgon!

Q: Which casino in Vegas do pirates love the most?

A: The Harrrrrrd Rock.

Q: What lies at the bottom of the ocean and twitches?

A: A nervous wreck.

Q: Where did the one-legged pirate go for breakfast?

A: IHOP.

Q: Do pirates like to fight?

A: Sword of.

Q: Why couldn't the crew play cards?

A: Because the captain was standing on the deck.

Q: Who did the ghost pirate hire to repair his boat?

A: A skeleton crew!

Q. What's the difference between a pirate and a cranberry farmer?

A. A pirate buries his treasure, but a cranberry farmer treasures his berries.

Q: How much rum does it take to make a pirate drunk?

A: A Galleon.

Q: What did the pirate's parrot say when it fell in love with a duck?

A: Polly wants a 'quacker.'

Q: What's the difference between a hungry pirate and a drunken pirate?

A: One has a rumbling tummy and the other's a tumbling rummy.

Q. How much does it cost for a pirate to get his ears pierced?

A. $2.00. That's a buck an ear.

Q: What happened when the pirate fell into the Red Sea?

A: He got marooned!

Q: What happened when the pirate heard a rumor that a group of skunks was going to sink his ship?

A: He fell for it hook, line and stinker.

Q: What happens when one pirate sees another pirate?

A: Pira-See!

Q: What happened to the pirate when his wooden leg caught fire?

A: He got burned to the ground.

How do?

Q: How do pirates know they exist?

A: Because they think and therefore they
ARRRRRR!

Q: How do pirates make their money?

A: By hook or by crook.

Q: How do pirates pay for a round o' rum down at the pub?

A: With Bar-Nickels!

Q: How do geriatric pirates get around?

A: With Davy Jones Walker.

Q: How do pirates prefer to communicate?

A: Aye to aye!

Q: What did one pirate say to the other?

A: "I sea you!"

Q: How do you save a dying pirate?

A: C-P-arrrrrrr

Q: How do pirates raise their children?

A: Stern-ly

Q: How do pirates like to cook their steaks?

A: On a Baaarbecue!

Why do?

Q: Why do doctors hate operating on pirates?

A: Because they have crossed bones!

Q: Why do pirates like killing zombies so much?

A: They are easy tarrrrrrrgets!

Q: Why do you never, ever see pirates crying?

A: They like their private-tears.

Q: Why do pirates bury their treasure 18 inches under the ground?

A: Because booty is only shin deep.

Q: Why do seagulls fly over the sea?

A: Because if they flew over the bay, they'd be bagels!

Q: Why do Pirates make the best singers?

A: They hit the high sea notes with ease.

What are?

Q: What are all pirate movies rated?

A: rrrrrrrrrrrrrr!

Q: What are pirate children afraid of?

A: The darrrrrrrrrrk.

Q: What are the pirate's favorite vowels?

A: AAAAA, EEEEEE, IIIIII, OOOOOO, UUUUUU, and sometimes Why.

Q: What are the pirate's least favorite vowels?

A: Marriage vows.

Q: What are the 10 letters of the pirate alphabet?

A: I, I, R, and the seven C's!

Q: Why are pirates called pirates?

A: Because they arrrr!

Why Don't

Q: Why don't pirates take a bath before they walk the plank?

A: Because they'll just wash up on shore later.

Q: Why don't pirates with a hook on their arm like helping others?

A: They find it extremely hard to lend a hand.

Q: Why don't pirates like traveling on mountain roads?

A: S'curvy.

Q: Why don't pirates go to strip clubs?

A: Because they already have plenty of booty.

Where do?

Q: Where do kid pirates like to go for fun?

A: To the arrgh-cade!

Q: Where do pirates buy pencils and sketch pads?

A: The arrrrrrt store.

Q. Where do pirates put their weapons?

A: In their enemies.

Q: Where do pirates put their trash?

A: The Garrrrrrrrrrrbage can.

Q: Where do pirates go for their haircuts?

A: To the barrrrrber.

Q: Who do Pirates call when they break their peg leg?

A: The Carrrrrrpenter.

Q: Where do pirates go out for dinner?

A: Long John Silver's!

What do?

Q: What do you call a pirate with no eyes?

A: A prate. Just a prate. Nothing else.

Q: What do you call a pirate with three eyes?

A: Piiirate!

Q. What would you call a pirate with 4 eyes?

A. iiiirate.

Q: What do you get when you cross a parrot and a shark?

A: A bird that will talk your head off.

Q: What do pirates wear in the winter?

A: Long Johns.

Q: What do you call a stupid pirate?

A: The pillage idiot.

Q: What do you call a pirate that skips class?

A: Captain Hooky.

Q: **What do you call a pirate that steals from the rich and gives to the poor?**

A: Robin hook!

Q: **What do pirates think happens at the end of time?**

A: Arrrrmageddon.

Q: What do pirates do for fun?

A: Have parrrrrrrrrties.

Q: What do you call a selfish pirate?

A: Extremely arrrrr-ogant.

Q: What do you call it when two pirates call it a draw?

A: A stale-matey!

Q: What do you call a pirate with two eyes and two legs?

A: A rookie.

Q: What do pirates do on Black Friday?

A: Shop the sails.

Q: What do pirate put on their toast?

A: Jelly Roger.

Q: What do you call a pirates sword that is completely blunt?

A: A cut-less.

What did?

Q: What did the pirate pay for his piercings?

A: Only a buck-an-ear. He got them on a sail.

Q: What did the pirate say during the winter storm?

A: Thar she snows!

Q: What did the pirate say to the banker?

A: Aye-ll have my own ship schooner or later.

Q: What did the pirate name his dog?

A: Patches!

Q: What did the pirate wear on Halloween?

A: A pumpkin patch

Q: What did the first mate see in the toilet?

A: The captain's log!

Q: What did the pirate say at his baby's gender reval?

A: It's a boy matey!

Q: What did the pirate say to his girlfriend?

A:"You are perfect just the way you Arrrrr!"

Q: What did the pirate's landlord say when he was evicted?

A: Get out, you free-looter!

Q: What do pirates eat on cold winter nights?

A: Hearrrrrty stews.

Q: What does a pirate eat for breakfast?

A: Captain Crunch

Q: What does a gourmet pirate add to the plate to make it look nice?

A: A Garrrrr-nish

Q: What did the pirate do after eating the beans?

A: Farrrrrrrt!

Q: What did the sea-police say when they arrested the pirate?

A: You're under a chest!

Q: What did the ocean say to the pirate?

A: Nothing, it just waved.

Q: What did the pirate get when he crossed a centipede and a parrot?

A: A walkie-talkie!

What's a?

Q: What's a buccaneer?

A: A high price to pay for corn.

Q: Which baseball team did the pirate play for?

A: The Pittsburgh Pirates

Q: What's a pirate's favorite baseball team?

A: It's Arrizona Diamondbacks. Real pirates don't live in cold places like Pittsburg.

Q: What's a pirate boxer's biggest strength?

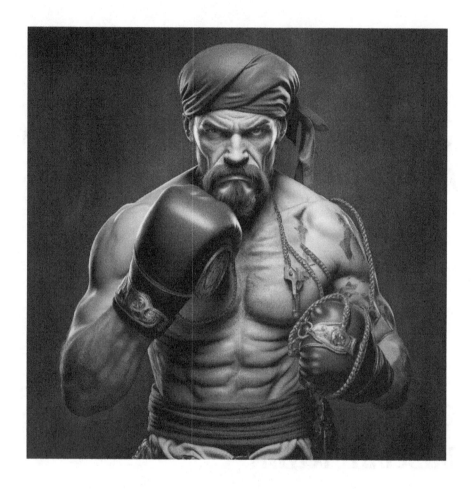

A: His left hook!

Q: What's a pirate's favorite country?

A: Arrrgentina.

Q: What's a pirate's favorite letter of the alphabet?

A: P, because it is like an Arrrr but it be missing a leg.

Q: What's a pirate's favorite element?

A: Aaarrrrgon, is not it, it's the element of surprise!

Q: What's a pirate's favorite food?

A: Arrrrrtichokes.

Q: What's a pirate's favorite doll?

A: A Baaaaaaarrrrrbie!

Q: What was the pirate's one legged girlfriend called?

A: Peggy!

Q. What's a pirate's favorite movie?

A. Booty and the Beast. (But it is arr-rated.)

Q: What's a pirate's favorite part of a song?

A: The hook!

Q: What does a pirate get when he crossed a cat with a parrot?

A: A carrot!

Q: **What's a pirate's favorite letter of the alphabet?**

A: R, unless he B at C.

Q: **What's a pirate's favorite kind of fish?**

A: A swordfish!

Q: What's a pirate's favorite restaurant?

A: Arrrrrbys.

Q: What's a pirate's favorite astronomer?

A: Arrrchimedies.

Q: What's a pirate's favorite music genre?

A: Arrrrrr & B.

Q: What's a pirate's favorite antibiotic?

A: Errrythromycin.

Q: What's a pirate's favorite mode of transportation?

A: Carrrrrrrr.

Q: What's a pirate's favorite sock?

A: Arrrgiles.

Q: What's a pirate's favorite math class in school?

A: Home economics. We fooled you!

Q: Why didn't the pirate kid like her arrithmatic class?

A: Because only 3.14% of all mathematicians are Pie-Rates.

Q: What's a pirate's favorite school subject?

A: Art. We told you they hate arrithmetic.

Q: What's a pirate's worst enemy?

A: Termites.

Q: What's a pirate's favorite basketball move?

A: The hook shot

Q: What's a pirate's favorite musical instrument?

A: The guit-arrrr

What does?

Q: What does a pirate dog do?

A: Scallywag his tail!

Q. What does the captain keep up his sleevie?

A. His armie.

Q: What does a pirate's phone ringer sound like?

A: Ringy dinghy dinghy.

Q: What does a pirate use a cell phone for?

A: Booty calls.

Q: What does a pirate name his dog?

A: The Plank. That's why he's always walking The Plank.

Q: What does a dyslexic pirate say?

A: RRAAHH!

Q: What does a pirate use to blow stuff up?

A: His M-80's.

Q: What does the pirate say when his leg gets stuck in the freezer?

A: Shiver me timbers!

How Did?

Q: How did the crabs get on the boat?

A: They came over on the captain's dinghy.

Q: How did the pirate find out he needed spectacles?

A: He took an aye exam!

Q. How does a pirate get to the top of the building?

A. By elevataaaaarrrrrrr!!!!!

Q: Why do pirates make great lawyers?

A: Because they're very skilled at arrrrrguing

Q: How did the pirate become a lawyer?

A: He passed the barrrrrrr exam.

Q: How did Captain Hook die?

A: Multiple stabbings. He got a bad case of an itchy rash.

Q: Blackbeard's friend Bluebeard was killed in battle, how did he bring him back to life?

A: With Sea Pee Arrrrgh.

Q: How did the pirate get his Jolly Roger flag so cheaply?

A: He bought it on sail.

Q: How did the pirate stop the computer hackers?

A: He installed a patch.

Why did

Q: Why did the pirate pull out of the stock market?

A: He was in shark-invested waters!

Q: Why did two pirates get into an argument?

A: Because they couldn't see aye to aye!

Q: Why did the captain wear a suit and tie?

A: He had a cor-pirate meeting.

Q: Why did the pirate join the gym?

A: To improve his booty.

Q: Why did the pirate like playing golf?

A: He was always under parrrrrrrr.

Q: Why did the pirate give up the game of golf?

A: He kept hooking the ball.

Q: Why did the pirate move to Russia?

A: To become a Czarrrr

Q: Why did the pirate go to the college?

A: To become an arrrrrchitect!

Q: Why did the pirate buy an eye patch?

A: Because he couldn't afford an iPad!

Q: Why did the pirate have to walk the plank?

A: Because he couldn't afford a dog.

Q: Why did the pirate confuse all of his Tinder dates?

A: They couldn't figure out if he was blinking or winking.

Q: Why did the shipwrecked pirate call his friend?

A: Because he trusted his friend-ship.

Q: Why did Bluebeard offend so many ladies?

A: He kept getting slapped each time he said yo-ho!

Q: Why did the pirate take his dog to the vet?

A: Because he had a scurvy dog.

Q: Why did the pirate divorce his wife?

A: They were arrrguing too much.

Q: Why did the pirate quit his plundering ways?

A: He was a peg leg in a square hole.

Q: Why did the pirate get lost?

A: He wasn't shore which way to go.

Why Are?

Q: Why are pirates always so healthy?

A: They get such a good dose of vitamin sea.

Q: Why are pirates afraid of the Dykes in New Orleans?

A: Because they arrre so big.

Q: Why are pirates so angry when they come back from the toilet?

A: After they get rid of the p they become irate.

Q: Why are math teachers secretly pirates?

A: Because they're always trying to find X!

Q: Who gets all their movies for free?

A: Pirates!

Q: Where's me Buccaneers?

A: Arrrg, they are on your buckin head Captain.

Q: Why is pirate poker so addictive?

A: Once ye lose yer first hand, ye get hooked!

Q: Which Star Wars character do pirates like the most?

A: Aarrrrggh-2-D-2.

Q: What was the name of Blackbeard's wife?

A: Peg.

Q: What did the teacher tell the pirate?

A: Mind your seas and q's.

Q: Where do pirates go on vacation?

A: Pirates don't need to go on vacation. They get all the arrr and arrr they need at work.

Q: What type of a haircut does a pirate get?
pirate get?

A: A crew cut!

Q: Is your wife messin around with your first mate?

A: Knot on my watch!

Q: What vegetable do pirates hate the most?

A: Leeks.

Pirate Jokes

Red Shirt

Long ago, when sailing ships ruled the waves, a captain and his crew were in danger of being boarded by a pirate ship. As the crew became frantic, the captain bellowed to his First Mate, "Bring me my red shirt!"

The First Mate quickly retrieved the captain's red shirt, which the captain put on, and led the crew to battle the pirate boarding party. Although some casualties occurred among the crew, the pirates were repelled. Later that day, the lookout screamed that there were two pirate vessels sending boarding parties. The crew cowered in fear, but the captain, calm as ever, bellowed, "Bring me my red shirt!"

Once again the battle was on. However, the Captain and his crew repelled both boarding parties, though this time more casualties occurred.

Weary from the battles, the men sat around on deck that night recounting the day's occurrences when an ensign looked to the Captain and asked, "Sir, why did you call for your red shirt before the battle?"

The Captain, giving the ensign a look that only a captain can give, exhorted, "If I am wounded in battle, the red shirt does not show the wound and thus, you men will continue to fight unafraid."

The men sat in silence marveling at the courage of such a man. As dawn came the next morning, the lookout screamed that there were pirate ships, 10 of them, all with boarding parties on their way.

The men became silent and looked to the Captain, their leader, for his usual command. The Captain, calm as ever, bellowed, "Bring me red shirt and me brown pants!"

The Crock

A man sees a pirate at a bar and asks him
how he got the hook hand. "Oh, I was leanin'
over the deck and a croc jumped out of the
water and bit off me hand!"

The man then asked him how he got the eye patch. "Oh, me and me mateys were sailin' on the sea when I looked up at a seagull flyin' above us, and the seagull pooped in me eye!"

Surprised, the man said, "Wow, a seagull dropping was powerful enough to take out your eye?!" The pirate laughed "Oh no. After the seagull pooped in my eye, I went to rub it. It was me first day with me hook!"

The Genie

A pirate and his first mate were adrift in a lifeboat following a dramatic escape from a valiant battle.

While rummaging through the boat's provisions, the pirate stumbled across an old lamp. Hoping that a Genie would appear, he rubbed the lamp vigorously. To the amazement of the castaways, a gorgeous Genie came forth.

The Genie said that she would grant him one wish. Without giving any thought to the matter the pirate blurted out, "Arrrgg, turn the entire ocean into rum!"

The Genie clapped her hands and with a deafening thunderbolt, the entire ocean turned into the finest rum ever made. As the pirate jumped in, the Genie vanished.

The next morning the gentle lapping of rum on the hull woke up the pirate. He opened his eyes to see his first mate with a disgusting look on his face. The pirate said to him "what's wrong, I didn't see you drink anything all night. The first mate responded, why did you pee in the ocean and not into the boat?

If The Ocean

Say the following in your best pirate voice:
If the ocean were whiskey and I were a duck,
I'd swim to the bottom and never come up,
But the ocean isn't whiskey and I'm not a duck,
So I think I will just sit here and get all -ucked
up.

I'm a pirate, off to sea! It's a plunderful life for me.

Seeing a pirate ship in person is truly oar-inspiring.

You can abso-loot-ley trust me with the treasure map.
All I Caribbean about is finding the treasure!

Pirates of the Carry On

Airport security caught me hiding a pirate in my luggage. They are going to make a movie about it called "pirates of the carry on".

The Bad Parrot

A pirate had stopped his pirating ways and mended his peace in the world. But his parrot was not willing to give up his plundering ways so easily. He was constantly swearing about the old days and refusing to behave.

After months of his parrot squawking profanities at him the ex-pirate finally had enough of it. All he could think of to do was to stick the poor guy in the freezer as punishment.

When the ex-pirate figured his friend had finally learned his lesson he let him out.

The parrot was very thankful and said: "I promise I'll be good now, no more swearing and mocking!

But can you please tell me what in the hell did the turkey do to you?"

A pirate Walks Into A Bar...

A pirate walks into a bar and he has a ship's wheel stuck on his crotch. "Arrr, give me a pint of yer strongest whiskey!" he says.

The bartender looks at him and asks him, "what happened? why have you got a ship's wheel stuck to your pants?"

The pirate says "ARRG me ship was a'tossin in a nor easter! Things got rough and we took a rouge wave on the bow and I snagged 'er on me wall nut sack. Ive tried and tried to get er off but I'm afraid it be stuck there forever."

The concerned bartender without thinking about it grabs the wheel and started twisting it to help get it off.

"Aaaaaar!" screams the pirate "stop it, yer driving me nuts!"

Pirate leftovers

A pirate walks into a bar.
It was at that moment that the pirate realized
that he was wearing his eye patch on the
wrong eye.

A pirate plunders the high seas. A pie-rat plunders the pantry.

A slice of apple pie is $2 in Jamaica and $3 in the Bahamas. These are the pie rates of the Caribbean.

The friendly pirate

A cruise ship passes by a remote island, all the passengers see a bearded man with an eye patch running around and waving his arms wildly. "Captain," one passenger asks, "who is that man over there?" "I have no idea," the captain says, "but he goes nuts every year when we pass him."

The thoughtful pirate

A pirate woman is in a fight with her husband. She says, "You never pay attention to me. You never listen to me, you don't care about anything I do and you never buy me flowers."

The pirate, thinking quickly says, "I will buy your flowers, how much do you want for them?

The Pirate Dermatologist

A pirate goes to a dermatologist to get some moles on his back checked out. When the lab tests come back the doctor smiles at him and says, "It's all ok, they're benign. The pirate stabs the doctor and says "you stupid idiot, there be ten of them."

Made in United States
Orlando, FL
10 January 2024

42322956R00083